Amber
the Orange
Fairy

Dedicated to Fiona Waters,
who has loved fairies
all her life

Special thanks to
Narinder Dhami

ISBN-13: 978-0-439-74465-2
ISBN-10: 0-439-74465-2

12 11 10 9 8 7   10 11 12/0

Printed in China

Amber
the Orange
Fairy

by Daisy Meadows

illustrated by Georgie Ripper

SCHOLASTIC INC.

New York Toronto London Auckland Sydney
Mexico City New Delhi Hong Kong Buenos Aires

The
Fairyland
Palace

Maze

Forest

Orchard

Black
Pot

Meadow

Tower

Beach

Tidepools

Rainspell Island

Cold winds blow and thick ice forms,
I conjure up this fairy storm.
To seven corners of the human world
the Rainbow Fairies will be hurled!

I curse every part of Fairyland,
with a frosty wave of my icy hand.
For now and always, from this day,
Fairyland will be cold and gray!

Ruby is safely hidden in the
pot at the end of the rainbow.
Now Rachel and Kirsty must find
Amber the Orange Fairy!
They don't have much time!

Contents

A Very Unusual Shell

"What a beautiful day!" Rachel Walker shouted, staring up at the blue sky. She and her friend Kirsty Tate were running along Rainspell Island's yellow, sandy beach. Their parents walked a little way behind them.

"It's a *magical* day," Kirsty added. The two friends smiled at each other.

Rachel and Kirsty had come to
Rainspell Island for their vacations.
But they soon found out it really
was a magical place!

As they ran, they passed tide pools
that sparkled like jewels in the sunshine.

Rachel spotted a little *splash!* in one of
the pools. "There's something in there,
Kirsty!" She pointed. "Let's go look."

The girls jogged over to the pool and
crouched down to see.

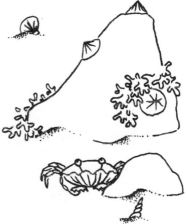

Kirsty's heart thumped as she gazed into the crystal-clear water. "What is it?" she asked.

Suddenly, the water rippled. A little brown crab scuttled sideways across the sandy bottom and disappeared under a rock.

Kirsty felt disappointed. "I thought it might be another Rainbow Fairy," she said.

"So did I." Rachel sighed. "Never mind. We'll keep looking."

"Of course we will," Kirsty agreed. Then she put her finger to her lips as their parents came up behind them. *"Shhh."*

Kirsty and Rachel had a big secret. They were helping to find the seven missing Rainbow Fairies. Jack Frost put a wicked spell on the fairies and trapped them on Rainspell Island. The Rainbow Fairies made Fairyland bright and colorful. Until they were all found, Fairyland would be dark and gray.

Rachel looked at the shimmering blue sea. "Do you want to go swimming?" she asked.

But Kirsty wasn't listening. She was shading her eyes with her hand and looking farther along the beach. "Look over there, Rachel — by those rocks," she said.

Then Rachel could see it, too — something glittering and sparkling in the sunshine. "Wait for me!" she

called, as Kirsty hurried down the
beach.

When they saw what it was, the two
friends sighed in disappointment.

"It's just the wrapper from a
chocolate bar," Rachel said sadly. She

bent down and picked up the shiny, purple foil.

Kirsty thought for a moment. "Do you remember what the Fairy Queen told us?" she asked.

Rachel nodded. *"Let the magic come to you,"* she said. "You're right, Kirsty. We should just enjoy our vacation, and wait for the magic to happen. After all, that's how we found Ruby in the pot at the end of the rainbow, isn't it?" She put

her beach bag down on the sand.
"Come on — race you to the water!"

They rushed into the water. The sea
was cold and salty, but the sun felt warm
on their backs. They waved at their
parents, sitting on the sand, and splashed
around in the waves until they got
goose bumps.

"Ow!" Kirsty gasped as they paddled
out of the water. "I just stepped on
something sharp."

"It might have been a shell,"
said Rachel. "There are lots
of them around here." She
picked up a pale pink one
and showed it to Kirsty.

"Let's see how many we can find,"
Kirsty said.

The two girls walked along the beach looking for shells. They found long, thin, blue shells and tiny, round, white shells. Soon their hands were full. They had walked right around the curve of the bay. Rachel looked over her shoulder and a sudden gust of wind whipped her hair across her face. "Look how far we've come," she said. Kirsty stopped. The wind blew at her back and made goose bumps stand out on her arms.

"It's getting cold now," she said.
"Should we go back?"

"Yes, it must be almost lunchtime,"
said Rachel.

The two girls began to walk back
along the beach. They'd only gone a
few steps when the wind suddenly
stoppcd.

"That's funny," said Kirsty. "It's not
windy here at all."

They looked back and saw perfect
little swirls of sand being lifted by the

wind. "Oh!" said Rachel, and the two friends looked at each other in excitement.

"It's magic," Kirsty whispered. "It just *has* to be!"

They walked back to where they had been, and the breeze swirled around their legs again. Then the golden sand at their feet began to drift gently to one side, as if invisible hands were pushing it away. A large scallop shell appeared. It was much bigger than the other shells on the beach. It was a light peach color with soft orange streaks, and it was tightly closed.

Quickly, the girls kneeled down on the sand, dropping the little shells from their hands. Kirsty was just about to pick up

the scallop shell when Rachel put out
her hand. "Listen," she whispered.

They both listened hard.

Rachel smiled when she heard the
sound again.

Inside the shell, a tiny voice hummed
softly. . . .

The Magic Feather

Very carefully, Rachel picked up the shell. It felt warm and smooth.

The humming stopped at once. "I should not be scared," said the tiny voice. "I just have to be brave, and help will come very soon."

Hummm...

Kirsty put her face close to the shell. "Hello," she whispered. "Is there a fairy in there?"

"Yes!" cried the voice. "I'm Amber the Orange Fairy! Can you get me out of here?"

"Of course we will," Kirsty promised. "My name is Kirsty, and my friend Rachel is here, too." She looked up at Rachel, her eyes shining. "We've found

another Rainbow Fairy!"

"Quick," Rachel said. "Let's get the shell open." She took hold of the scallop shell and tried to pull the two halves apart. Nothing happened.

"Try again," said
Kirsty. She and Rachel
each grabbed one half
of the shell and tugged.
But the shell stayed
tightly shut.

"What's happening?"
Amber asked. She sounded worried.

"We can't open the shell," Kirsty said.
"But we'll think of something." She
turned to Rachel. "If we find a piece of
driftwood, maybe we can use it to pry
open the shell."

Rachel glanced around the beach.
"I don't see any driftwood," she said.
"We could try tapping the shell
on a rock."

"But that might hurt Amber," Kirsty
pointed out.

Suddenly, Rachel remembered something. "What about the magic bags the Fairy Queen gave us?" she said.

"Of course!" Kirsty cried. She put her face close to the shell again. "Amber, we're going to look in our magic bags," she said.

"OK, but please hurry," Amber called. Rachel opened her beach bag. The two magic bags were hidden under her towel. One of the bags was glowing with a golden light. Carefully, Rachel pulled it out. "Look," she whispered to Kirsty. "This one is all lit up."

"Open it, quick," Kirsty whispered back.

As Rachel untied the bag, a fountain of glittering sparks flew out.

"What's inside?" Kirsty asked, gently putting down the shell.

Rachel slid her hand into the bag. She could feel something light and soft. She pulled it out, scattering sparkles everywhere. It was a shimmering golden feather.

Kirsty and Rachel stared at the feather.

"It's really pretty," said Kirsty. "But what are we going to *do* with it?"

"I don't know," Rachel replied. She tried to use the feather to push the two halves of the shell apart. But the feather just curled up in her hand. "Maybe we should ask Amber."

"Amber, we've looked in the magic bags," Kirsty said, "and we found a feather."

"Oh, good!" Amber said happily from inside the shell. "That's wonderful news!"

"But we don't know what to do with it," Rachel added.

Amber laughed. It sounded like the tinkle of a tiny bell. "You tickle the shell, of course!" she said.

"Do you think that will work?" Rachel said to Kirsty.

"Let's give it a try," Kirsty said.

Rachel began to tickle the shell with the feather. At first nothing happened. Then they heard a soft, gritty chuckle, followed by a tinkly giggle from inside the shell.

Then another chuckle, and another. Slowly, the two halves of the shell began to open.

"It's working." Kirsty gasped. "Keep tickling, Rachel!"

The shell was laughing hard now. The two halves opened wider. . . . And there, sitting inside the smooth, peach-colored shell, was Amber the Orange Fairy.

A Stranger in the Pot

"I'm free!" Amber cried joyfully.

She shot out of the shell and up into
the air, her wings fluttering in a
rainbow-colored blur. Orange fairy
dust floated down around Kirsty and
Rachel. It turned into orange bubbles as
it fell. One of the bubbles landed on
Rachel's arm and burst with a tiny *pop!*

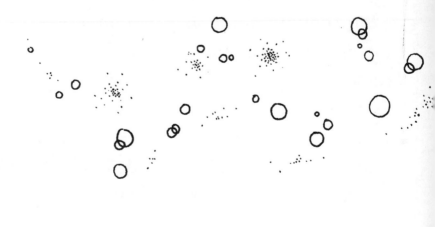

"The bubbles smell like oranges!" Rachel said with a smile.

Amber spun through the sky, turning cartwheels one after the other. "Thank you!" she called. Then she swooped down toward Rachel and Kirsty.

She wore a shiny orange leotard and tall boots. Her brown hair was held in a high ponytail, tied with a band of peach blossoms. In her hand was an orange wand tipped with gold.

"I'm so glad you found me!" Amber shouted. She landed on Rachel's shoulder, then cartwheeled lightly across to Kirsty's. "But who are you? And where are my Rainbow sisters? And what's happening in Fairyland? How am I going to get back there?"

She was talking so fast that Kirsty and Rachel couldn't get a word in.

Suddenly, Amber stopped. She floated down and landed softly on Rachel's hand. "I'm sorry," she said with a smile. "But I haven't had anyone to talk to. I've been trapped in that shell ever since Jack Frost's spell banished us from Fairyland. How did you know where to find me?"

"Kirsty and I promised your sister Ruby that we would look for all the Rainbow Fairies," Rachel told her.

"Ruby?" Amber's face lit up. She spun around on Rachel's hand. "You've found Ruby?"

"Yes, she's safe now," Rachel said. "She's in the pot at the end of the rainbow."

Amber did a happy backflip. "Please take me to her!" she begged.

"I'll ask our parents if we can go for a walk," Kirsty said. And she ran off across the beach.

"Do you know what's happening in Fairyland?" Amber asked Rachel.

Rachel nodded. She and Kirsty had flown to Fairyland with Ruby. Ruby had used her wand to shrink them to fairy size, and she had given them magical fairy wings. "King Oberon and Queen Titania miss you very much," Rachel told Amber. "With no color, Fairyland is a sad place."

Amber's wings drooped.

Kirsty was hurrying back toward them. "Mom said we can go for a walk," she panted.

"Well, what are we waiting for? Let's go!" Amber called. She flew up and did a somersault in midair. Rachel pulled their shorts, T-shirts, and sneakers out of her beach bag and both girls put them on. "Rachel, could you bring my shell?" Amber asked. Rachel looked surprised. "Yes, if you want," she said.

Amber nodded. "It's really comfy," she explained. "It will make a lovely bed for me and my sisters."

Rachel put the shell in her beach bag, and they set off, with Amber sitting cross-legged on Kirsty's shoulder.

"My wings are a bit stiff after being in the shell for so long," she told them. "I don't think I can fly very far yet."

The girls followed the path to the clearing in the woods where the pot at the end of the rainbow was hidden.

"Here we are," said Rachel. "The pot is right over there." She stopped. The pot was where they'd left it — under the

weeping willow tree. But climbing out
of it was a big, green frog.

"Oh, no!" Rachel gasped. She and
Kirsty stared at the frog in horror.

Where was Ruby?

Home Sweet Home

Rachel dashed forward and grabbed the frog around his plump, green tummy.

The frog turned his head and glared at her, his eyes bulging. "And what do you think *you're* doing?" he croaked.

Rachel was so shocked, she let go of the frog. He hopped away from her, looking very annoyed.

"It's a talking frog!" Kirsty gasped, her eyes wide. "And it looks like it's wearing glasses. . . ."

"Bertram!" Amber flew down from Kirsty's shoulder. "I didn't know it was you."

Bertram bowed his head as Amber hugged him. "Thank goodness you're safe, Miss Amber!" he said happily. "And may I say, it's very good to see you again."

Amber beamed at Rachel and Kirsty. "Bertram isn't an ordinary frog, you know," she explained. "He's one of King Oberon's footmen. He works closely with the king and queen."

"Oh, yes!" said Kirsty. "I remember now. We saw the frog footmen when we went to Fairyland with Ruby."

"But they were wearing uniforms then," Rachel added.

"Excuse me, miss, but a frog in a uniform would *not* be a good idea on Rainspell Island," Bertram pointed out.

"It's much better if I look like an ordinary frog."

"But what are you doing here, Bertram?" asked Amber. "And where's Ruby?"

"Don't worry, Miss Amber," Bertram replied. "Miss Ruby is safe in the pot." He suddenly looked very stern. "King Oberon sent me to Rainspell. The Cloud Fairies spotted Jack Frost's goblins sneaking out of Fairyland. We think he has sent them here to stop you from finding the Rainbow Fairies."

Kirsty felt a shiver run down down her spine. "Jack Frost's goblins?" she said.

"They're his servants," Amber explained. Her wings trembled

and she looked very scared. "They want
to keep Fairyland cold and gray!"

"Never fear, Miss Amber!" Bertram
croaked. "I'm here to look after you and
keep the Rainbow Fairies safe."

Suddenly, a shower of red fairy dust
shot out of the pot. Ruby fluttered out.
"I heard voices," she shouted joyfully.

"Amber! I *knew* it was you!"

"Ruby!" Amber called. And then she cartwheeled through the air toward her sister.

Rachel and Kirsty watched as the two fairies flew into each other's arms. The air around them fizzed with little red flowers and orange bubbles.

"Thank you, Kirsty and Rachel," said Ruby. She and Amber floated down to them, holding hands. "It's so good to have Amber back safely."

"What about you?" Rachel asked. "Have you been OK in the pot?"

Ruby nodded. "I'm fine now that Bertram is here," she replied. "And I've been making the pot into a fairy home. We can stay there until all our fairy sisters are found."

"I brought my shell with me," Amber said. "It will make a lovely bed for us. Could you show her, Rachel?"

Rachel put her bag down on the grass and took the peach-colored shell out of it.

"It's beautiful," said Ruby. Then she smiled at Rachel and Kirsty. "Would you like to come and see our new home?" she asked.

"But the pot's much too small for Kirsty and me to fit inside," Rachel began. Then she started to tingle with excitement. "Oh! Are you going to make us fairy size again?"

Ruby nodded. She and Amber flew over the girls' heads, showering them with fairy dust. Rachel and Kirsty started to shrink, just as they had before. Soon they were the same size as Ruby and Amber.

"I *love* being a fairy," Kirsty said happily. She twisted around to look at her silvery wings.

"Me, too," Rachel agreed. She was getting used to seeing flowers as tall as trees!

Bertram hopped over to the pot. "I'll wait outside," he croaked.

"Come this way," said Ruby. She took Rachel's hand, and Amber took Kirsty's. Then the fairies led them toward the pot.

Rachel and Kirsty fluttered through

the air, dodging a butterfly that was
as big as they were. Its wings
felt like velvet as
they brushed
gently past it.

"I'm getting
better at flying!"
Kirsty said as she
landed neatly on
the edge of the pot.
She looked down eagerly.

The pot was full of sunlight. There

were little chairs made from twigs tied
with blades of grass. Each chair had a
cushion made from a soft, red berry.
Rugs of bright green leaves covered
the floor.

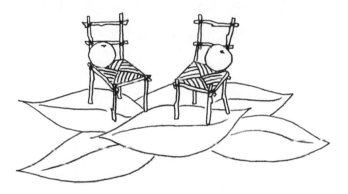

"Should we bring in the shell?" asked
Rachel.

The others thought this was a very
good idea. When they flew out of the
pot, Bertram was already pushing the
shell across the grass toward them.

"Here you are," he croaked.

The shell seemed very heavy now that Rachel and Kirsty were the same size as Ruby and Amber. But Bertram helped them lift it into the pot. Soon the shell bed sat neatly inside.

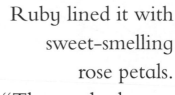

Ruby lined it with sweet-smelling rose petals.

"The pot looks lovely," Rachel said.

"I wish I could live here, too!" said Kirsty.

Ruby turned to her sister. "Do *you* like it, Amber?" she asked.

"It's beautiful," Amber replied. "It reminds me of our house back in Fairyland. I wish I could see Fairyland again. I miss it so much."

Ruby smiled. "Well, we can't go back to Fairyland for good until we're all together," she explained. "But I can *show* you Fairyland. Follow me!"

Bertram was still on guard next to the pot when they flew outside again. "Where are

you going, Miss Ruby?" he croaked.

"To the magic pond," Ruby replied. "Come with us." She sprinkled her magic dust over Rachel and Kirsty. Quickly, they grew back to their normal size. They went over to the pond.

Ruby flew above the water, scattering fairy dust. Just like before, a picture began to appear.

"Fairyland!" Amber cried, gazing into
the water.

Rachel and Kirsty watched, too.
Fairyland still looked sad and chilly. The

palace, the toadstool houses, the flowers, and the trees were all icy and gray.

Suddenly, a cold breeze rippled the surface of the water, and the picture started to fade.

"What's happening?" Kirsty whispered.

Everyone stared down at the pond. Another picture was taking shape — a thin, grinning face with frosty white hair and icicles hanging from his beard.

"Jack Frost!" Ruby gasped in horror. As she spoke, the air turned icy cold and the edges of the pool began to freeze.

"What's happening?" Rachel asked, shivering.

Bertram hopped forward. "This is bad news," he said. "It means that Jack Frost's goblins must be close by!"

Goblin Alert!

Rachel and Kirsty felt shivers run down their spines as the whole pond froze over. Jack Frost's grinning face faded away.

"Follow me," ordered Bertram. He hopped over to a large bush. "We'll hide here."

"Maybe we should go back to the pot," said Ruby.

"Not if the goblins are close by," Bertram replied. "We can't let them know where the pot is."

The two girls crouched down behind the bush next to Bertram. Ruby and Amber sat very still on Kirsty's shoulder. It was getting colder and colder. Rachel and Kirsty couldn't stop their teeth from chattering.

"What are the goblins like?" Rachel asked.

"They're bigger than us," said Amber. She was trembling with fear.

"And they have mean faces and long noses and big feet," Ruby added, holding her sister's hand for comfort.

"Hush, Miss Ruby," Bertram croaked. "I hear something."

Rachel and Kirsty listened. Suddenly, Rachel saw a long-nosed shadow dash across the clearing toward them. She grabbed Kirsty's arm. They were peering out of the bush when the leaves rustled right next to them. The two girls almost jumped out of their skin.

"Hey!" said a gruff voice, sounding very close. "What do you think you're doing?" Rachel and Kirsty held their breath.

"Nothing," said another gruff voice, rudely.

"Goblins!" Amber whispered in Kirsty's ear.

"You stepped on my toe," said the first goblin angrily.

"No, I didn't," snapped the other goblin.

"Yes, you did! Keep your big feet to yourself!"

"Well, at least my nose isn't as big as yours!"

The bush shook even more. It
sounded like the goblins were pushing
and shoving each other.

"Get out of my way!" one of them
shouted. "Ow!"

"That'll teach you to push *me*!" yelled
the other one.

Rachel and Kirsty looked at each
other in alarm. What if the goblins
found them there?

"Come on," puffed one of the goblins. "Jack Frost will be really angry if we don't find these fairies. You know he wants us to keep them from getting back to Fairyland."

"Well, they're not here, are they?" grumbled the other. "Let's try somewhere else."

The voices died away. The leaves stopped rustling. And suddenly, the air felt warm again. There was a cracking sound as the frozen pond began to melt.

"They're gone," Bertram croaked. "Quick, we must get back to the pot."

They all hurried across the clearing. The pot stood under the weeping willow tree, just as before.

"I'll stay outside in case the goblins come back," Bertram began. But a shout from Kirsty stopped them all in their tracks.

"Look!" she cried. "The pot's frozen over!"

Kirsty was right. The top of the pot was covered with a thick sheet of ice. No one, not even a fairy, could get inside.

Bertram to the Rescue

"Oh, no!" Ruby gasped. "The goblins must have been really close. Thank goodness they didn't discover the pot."

She flew over to the pot with Amber right behind her. They drummed on the ice with their tiny fists. But it was too thick for them to break through.

"Should *we* try, Rachel?" asked Kirsty.

"Maybe we could smash the ice with a stick."

But Bertram had another idea. "Stand back, please, everyone," he said.

The girls moved to the edge of the clearing. Ruby sat on Kirsty's hand, and Amber flew over to Rachel. They all watched.

Suddenly, Bertram took a mighty hop forward. He jumped right at the sheet of ice, kicking out with his webbed feet. But the ice did not break. "Let's try again," he panted.

He jumped forward
again and hit the ice.
This time, there was a
loud cracking sound. After
one more jump, the ice
shattered into little pieces.
Some of it fell inside the pot.
Rachel and Kirsty rushed over
to fish out the pieces of ice
before they melted.

"There you are," Bertram croaked.

"Thank you, Bertram," Ruby called.
She and Amber flew down and hugged
the frog.

Bertram looked pleased. "Just doing
my job, Miss Ruby," he said. "You and
Miss Amber must stay very close to the
pot from now on. It's dangerous for you
to go too far."

"We've got to say
good-bye to our friends
first," Amber told him.
She flew into the air and
did a backflip, smiling at
Rachel and Kirsty. "Thank you
a thousand times."

"We'll see you again soon," said
Rachel.

"When we've found your next
Rainbow sister," Kirsty added.

"Good luck!" said Ruby. "We'll be
waiting here for you. Come on,

Amber." She took her
sister's hand, and they
flew over to the pot.
The two fairies turned
to wave at the girls.
Then they disappeared inside.

"Don't worry," Bertram said. "I'll look after them."

"We know you will," Rachel said as she picked up her beach bag. She and Kirsty walked out of the woods. "I'm glad Ruby isn't on her own anymore," said Rachel. "Now she has Amber *and* Bertram."

"I didn't like those goblins," Kirsty said with a shudder. "I hope they don't come back again."

The girls made their way back to the beach. Their parents were packing up their towels. Rachel's dad saw Rachel and Kirsty coming down the path and went to meet them. "You've been gone a long time." He smiled. "We were just coming to look for you."

"Are we going home now?" Rachel asked.

Mr. Walker nodded. "It's very strange," he said. "It's suddenly turned quite chilly."

As he spoke, a cold breeze swirled
around Rachel and Kirsty. The friends
shivered and looked up at the sky. The
sun had disappeared behind a thick,
black cloud. The trees swayed in the
wind, and the leaves rustled as if they
were whispering to one another.

"Jack Frost's goblins are still here!"
Kirsty whispered.

"You're right," Rachel agreed. "Let's
hope Bertram can keep Ruby and
Amber safe while we look for the other
Rainbow Fairies."

Kirsty nodded and smiled at Rachel.
They still had five fairies to find. It
would take some magic and a lot of
work, but she was sure they could do it
together!

THE RAINBOW FAIRIES

Ruby and Amber have
been rescued. Now it's
time to search for

Sunny the Yellow Fairy!

But where could she be?
Join Kirsty and Rachel's adventure in
this special sneak peek. . . .

A Very Fierce Bee

"Over here, Kirsty!" called Rachel Walker. Kirsty ran across one of the emerald-green fields that covered this part of Rainspell Island. Buttercups and daisies dotted the grass.

"Don't go too far!" Kirsty's mom called. She and Kirsty's dad were climbing over a fence at the edge of the field.

Kirsty caught up with her friend. "What did you find, Rachel? Is it another Rainbow Fairy?" she asked hopefully.

"I don't know." Rachel was standing on the bank of a rippling stream. "I thought I heard something."

Kirsty's face lit up. "Maybe there's a fairy in the stream?"

Rachel nodded. She knelt down on the soft grass and put her ear close to the water.

Kirsty crouched down, too, and listened really hard.

The sun glittered on the water as it splashed over big, shiny pebbles. Tiny rainbows flashed and sparkled in the light — red, orange, yellow, green, blue, indigo, and violet.

And then they heard a tiny bubbling voice. "Follow me. . . ." it gurgled. "Follow me. . . ."

"Oh!" Rachel gasped. "Did you hear that?"

"Yes," said Kirsty, her eyes wide. "It must be a *magic* stream!"

Rachel felt her heart beat fast. "Maybe the stream will lead us to the Yellow Fairy," she said.

Rachel and Kirsty had a special secret. They had promised the king and queen of Fairyland that they would find the lost Rainbow Fairies. Jack Frost's spell had hidden the Rainbow Fairies on Rainspell Island. Fairyland would be cold and gray until all seven fairies had been found and returned to their home.

Silver fish darted in and out of the bright green weeds at the bottom of the stream. "Follow us, follow us. . . ." they whispered in tinkling voices.

Rachel and Kirsty smiled at each other. Titania, the Fairy Queen, had said that the magic would find them!

Kirsty's parents came up behind the girls and stopped to admire the stream, too. "Which way now?" asked Mr. Tate. "You two seem to know where you're going."

"Let's go this way," Kirsty said, pointing along the bank.

A brilliant bluebird flew up from its perch on a twig. Butterflies as bright as jewels fluttered among the cattails.

"Everything on Rainspell Island is so beautiful," said Kirsty's mom. "I'm glad we still have five days of vacation left!"

Yes, Rachel thought, *and five Rainbow Fairies still to find: Sunny, Fern, Sky, Inky, and Heather!*

Read the rest of

THE RAINBOW FAIRIES

Sunny the Yellow Fairy
to find out where the magic stream
leads Rachel and Kirsty.

RAINBOW magic™

There's Magic in Every Series!

The Rainbow Fairies

The Weather Fairies

The Jewel Fairies

The Pet Fairies

The Fun Day Fairies

The Petal Fairies

The Dance Fairies

The Music Fairies

The Sports Fairies

The Party Fairies

Read them all!

■ SCHOLASTIC

www.scholastic.com

www.rainbowmagiconline.com

HiT entertainment

RMFAIRY2